EXTINCT ANIMALS

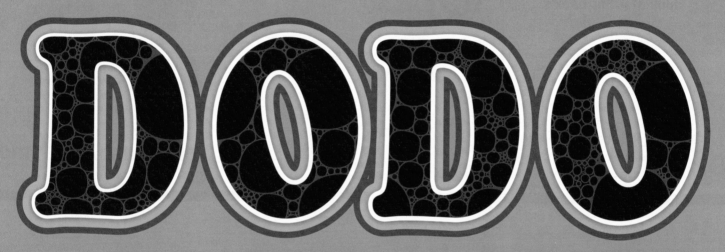

DODO

Aaron Carr

www.av2books.com

LET'S READ
AV²
BY WEIGL™
ADDED VALUE • AUDIO VISUAL

Go to www.av2books.com, and enter this book's unique code.

BOOK CODE

S 6 5 8 4 8 6

AV² by Weigl brings you media enhanced books that support active learning.

AV² provides enriched content that supplements and complements this book. Weigl's AV² books strive to create inspired learning and engage young minds in a total learning experience.

Your AV² Media Enhanced books come alive with...

 Audio
Listen to sections of the book read aloud.

 Video
Watch informative video clips.

 Embedded Weblinks
Gain additional information for research.

 Try This!
Complete activities and hands-on experiments.

 Key Words
Study vocabulary, and complete a matching word activity.

 Quizzes
Test your knowledge.

 Slide Show
View images and captions, and prepare a presentation.

... and much, much more!

Published by AV² by Weigl
350 5th Avenue, 59th Floor
New York, NY 10118

Websites: www.av2books.com   www.weigl.com

Library of Congress Control Number: 2014958629
ISBN 978-1-4896-3078-0 (hardcover)
ISBN 978-1-4896-3079-7 (softcover)
ISBN 978-1-4896-3080-3 (single-user eBook)
ISBN 978-1-4896-3081-0 (multi-user eBook)

Printed in the United States of America in Brainerd, Minnesota
1 2 3 4 5 6 7 8 9 0   19 18 17 16 15

022015
WEP021315

Project Coordinator: Aaron Carr
Art Director: Terry Paulhus

All illustrations by Jon Hughes, pixel-shack.com.

EXTINCT ANIMALS

DODO

In this book, you will learn

what its name means

what it looked like

where it lived

what it ate

and much more!

Meet the dodo.
Its name may have
meant "silly."

Dodos were large birds.

They were a little bigger than turkeys.

Dodos had two small wings.
They could not fly
with these small wings.

9

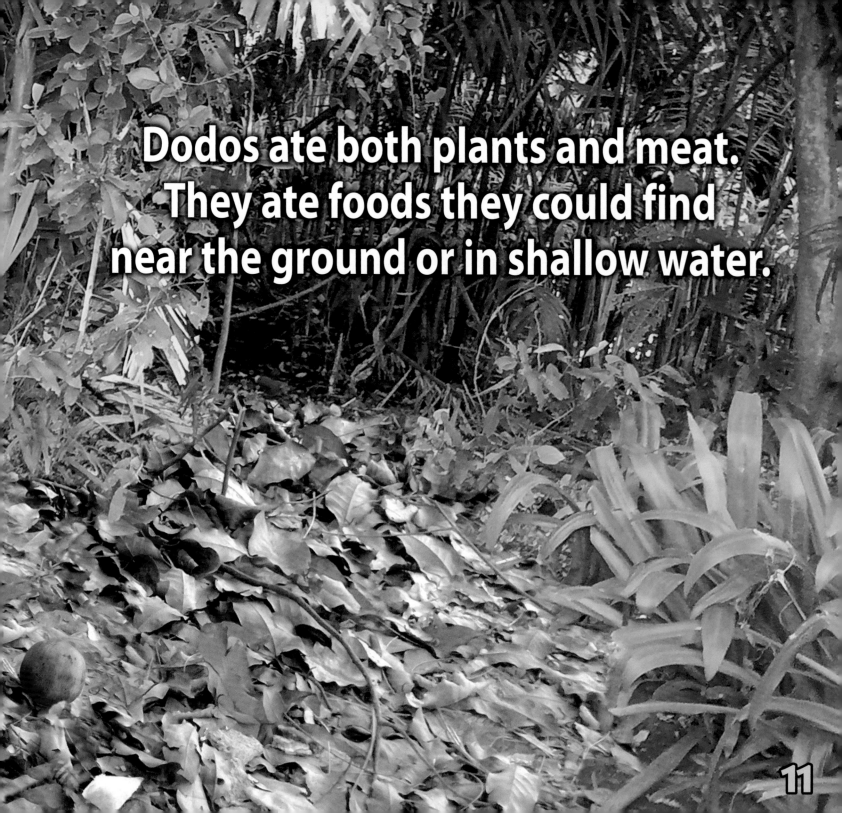

Dodos ate both plants and meat. They ate foods they could find near the ground or in shallow water.

Dodos had long hooked beaks.
They used their hooked beaks
to catch fish.

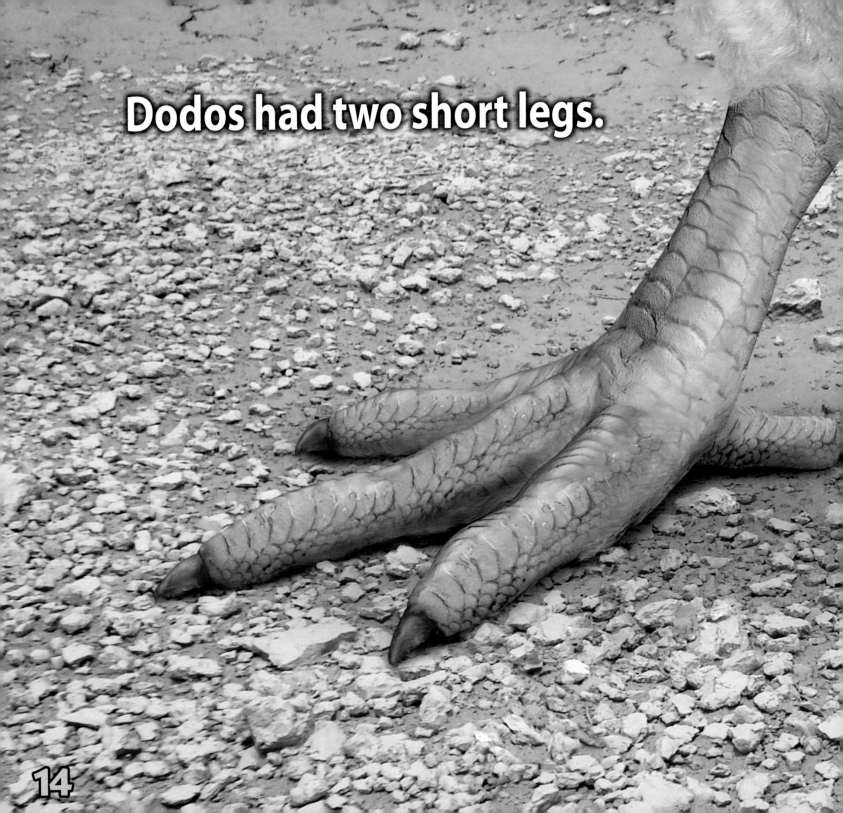

Dodos had two short legs.

They could run very fast on these short legs.

Dodos lived on an island
near Africa. This island
was covered in forest.

Dodos died out
more than 300 years ago.

People who saw dodos drew pictures of them.

White dodo or solitaire
Raphus solitaire

Today, people can go to museums to learn more about the dodo.

DODO FACTS

These pages provide detailed information that expands on the interesting facts found in the book. They are intended to be used by adults as a learning support to help young readers round out their knowledge of each amazing animal featured in the *Extinct Animals* series.

Pages 4–5

The name *dodo* may have meant "silly." Dodo may come from an old Portuguese word, *doudo*, meaning "simpleton," "foolish," or "silly." The first people to meet the dodo did not understand its behavior. This led to a belief that the dodo was odd or unintelligent. The bird was first named by Dutch travelers, who named it *walghvodel*, or "disgusting bird," in reference to its taste. By the end of the 1600s, the dodo had as many as 78 names in various languages. Its scientific name is *Raphus cucullatus*, which is Latin for "hooded bustard." A bustard is a large bird.

Pages 6–7

Dodos were larger than turkeys. The dodo stood about 3 feet (1 meter) tall and may have weighed as much as 50 pounds (23 kilograms). It was covered in feathers, with the exception of its face and lower legs. The dodo has been known as a plump bird throughout much of the past 300 years. However, a recent study indicated the bird may have been more streamlined through the neck, chest, and stomach than previously thought. The dodo's closest living relative is the pigeon.

Pages 8–9

Dodos had tiny wings that could not support flight. Like other flightless birds, dodos likely lost the ability to fly over time. Until humans arrived, dodos did not have any natural enemies, making flight unnecessary. In 1598, Dutch Vice Admiral Wybrand van Warwijck wrote one of the first records of a dodo sighting. He wrote that the birds did not appear to have wings, just three or four feathers sticking out where the wings should be.

Pages 10–11

Dodos were omnivores. The dodo's main foods were fruit, seeds, and fish. To help them digest their food, dodos swallowed rocks. This may have led to the early belief that dodos were not intelligent as explorers did not understand the role the rocks played in the dodo's digestion. Dodos also ate the fruit of the Calvaria major, or dodo, tree. The fruit would ripen and fall to the ground for dodos to eat. Dodos then spread the seeds in their droppings, helping the tree survive. These trees are now in danger of extinction without dodos to spread their seeds.

Pages 12–13

Dodos had long, hooked beaks. The dodo's beak was about 9 inches (23 centimeters) long. The beak was thick and became wider and more rounded near the tip. It ended in a pointed, downward hook. The main part of the beak was yellow or green according to early reports. The hooked end of the beak was a darker brown or blackish color. The dodo's powerful beak provided the bird with its method of fishing, gathering food, and self-defense.

Pages 14–15

Dodos could move quickly on two short, legs. Only the dodo's upper legs were covered in feathers. The lower legs were bare. Each foot had three forward-facing toes and one rear-facing toe. Each toe had a short claw. The rear toes may have acted like thumbs to allow dodos to grip objects. Early records of dodo sightings include several accounts of the birds running very quickly. The dodo's short legs, in comparison with the rest of its body, may have added to the belief that it was a slow, portly bird when it likely was not.

Pages 16–17

Dodos lived on an island near Africa. The dodo was only found on the island of Mauritius. This is a small island in the Indian Ocean, about 500 miles (800 kilometers) east of Madagascar. Mauritius has a subtropical climate that stays warm throughout the year. The island was mostly covered in forest at one time, but today much of its original forest is gone. Mauritius is home to a wide range of animals, including birds, insects, and small mammals, such as mongooses.

Pages 18–19

Dodos died out more than 300 years ago. The dodo has become a symbol of extinction and the role humans play in the loss of species. The dodo's extinction was one of the first widely known to be human-caused. Sailors and early settlers on Mauritius hunted dodos for food. They also brought animals such as dogs, cats, rats, and monkeys to the island. This, combined with rapid loss of habitat from deforestation, strained the dodo population. It is believed European sailors first encountered the dodo in about 1507. By 1681, the dodo was extinct.

Pages 20–21

People can go to museums to learn more about the dodo. Each year, millions of people visit museums around the world to see dodo fossils and life-sized recreations. Most museums use recreations since very few dodo fossils have been discovered. Several museums around the world have fossilized bones, feet, or skulls, but very few have complete, or even nearly completely, skeletons. The Natural History Museum in London, England, is one of the few with a nearly complete fossil.

KEY WORDS

Research has shown that as much as 65 percent of all written material published in English is made up of 300 words. These 300 words cannot be taught using pictures or learned by sounding them out. They must be recognized by sight. This book contains 51 common sight words to help young readers improve their reading fluency and comprehension. This book also teaches young readers several important content words, such as proper nouns. These words are paired with pictures to aid in learning and improve understanding.

Page	Sight Words First Appearance
4	its, have, may, name, the
6	large, were
7	a, little, than, they
9	could, had, not, small, these, two, with
11	and, both, could, find, foods, in, near, or, plants, water
12	long, their, used
15	on, run, very
16	an, lived, this, was
18	more, out, years
19	of, people, pictures, saw, them, who
20	about, can, go, learn

Page	Content Words First Appearance
4	dodo
6	birds
7	turkeys
8	wings
11	ground, meat
12	beaks, fish
14	legs
16	Africa, forest, island
21	museums